Everything You Need to Know About

STRESS

Most people experience some stress in their daily routine.

Everything You Need to Know About
STRESS

Eleanor H. Ayer

THE ROSEN PUBLISHING GROUP, INC.
NEW YORK

Published in 1994, 1998 by The Rosen Publishing Group, Inc.
29 East 21st Street, New York, NY 10010

Library of Congress Cataloging-in-Publication Data

Ayer, Eleanor
    Everything you need to know about stress / Eleanor H. Ayer
       p.   cm.
    Includes bibliographical references and index.
    ISBN 0-8239-2628-1
    1. Stress (Psychology)—Juvenile literature. 2. Stress management—Juvenile literature. [1. Stress (Psychology). 2. Stress management.] I. Title.
    BF575.S75A94 1994
    155.9'042—dc20
                                        94-434
                                            CIP
                                            AC

Manufactured in the United States of America

Contents

Introduction   6

1. Can You Live with Stress and
     Be Happy?   9

2. At Risk for Stress   15

3. How to Tell When You're
     Stressed Out   19

4. Learning About Stressors   27

5. Dealing with Your Stressor(s)   33

6. Reducing Stress by Changing
     Your Behavior   37

7. Mind Over Matter   43

8. Relieving Stress Through Your Body   49

9. You're in Control   56

Glossary   59

Where to Go for Help   61

For Further Reading   62

Index   63

Introduction

Do you worry for weeks about taking a test? Are you afraid to try out for the school's soccer team because you just know you'll fall flat on your face in front of everyone? Do you dread the sound of your parents fighting every night? Have you recently moved or changed schools? Do you avoid spending time alone with your boyfriend or girlfriend because he or she wants the relationship to go further than you do?

If you have faced any of these situations, or situations like these, you are all too familiar with stress.

Nature's Alarm System

Our bodies are equipped with a natural alarm system that once helped us prepare to fight or run from danger. That alarm system is called stress.

Thousands of years ago, the dangers peopled faced were obvious and life-threatening—an attacking animal, long winter months without food, or traveling through unknown, unexplored territories. When a person felt stress, it was because his or her life was threatened. He or she could either choose to fight for his or her life, or run to safety.

Today, however, the dangers that people face are not always as obvious or as simple. People, especially teens, live in a world of stress. School, family, friends, peer pressure, and a million other things add to the pressures of daily life. Some people deal with stress well. Others have a more difficult time with it.

Understanding that stress is a natural, permanent part of life is the first step toward learning how to cope with it. This book will explain many of the causes of stress, the effects of stress on people, and ways to handle the stress in your life. Although stress will always be a part of your life, it doesn't have to be the biggest part of it.

Some students do their best work under pressure.

Chapter 1

Can You Live with Stress and Be Happy?

*M*alcolm was a great basketball player. He played pick-up games at the park every weekend, and his team almost always won. One Saturday, Malcolm decided that he would try out for the school's basketball team that year. They had never won a championship, and Malcolm knew he could help them.

But as the tryouts drew closer, Malcolm became more and more nervous. His palms got sweaty and his heart began to race just thinking about playing in front of the coach and the team. "What if I don't catch a pass?" he thought to himself. "Or I miss a basket? Or I mess up a drill? I can't do it."

The morning of the tryouts, Malcolm had a headache and felt sick. He decided that he was too sick to try out for the team.

Good Self-Esteem

Malcolm had low self-esteem. He didn't believe that
he could do well under pressure, so he didn't even try.
In the end, Malcolm, and the team, lost out.

The sweaty palms and racing heart were Malcolm's
body's way of telling him that he was feeling stress
about the tryouts. But rather than dealing with the
stress, Malcolm let it take over.

One of the best ways to keep stress from taking
over is by having good self-esteem. Having good self-
esteem means believing in yourself. It means having
the confidence to work through the stress and nervous
feelings you have about something, and doing it anyway.

Your Stress Is Your Own

Different people are stressed by different things.
Although Malcolm was too stressed to try out for the
basketball team, he couldn't understand why his
friend, Jim, refused to play games at the park. Jim was
too nervous to play in front of his friends.

Megan liked being the chairperson for two clubs,
taking advanced classes, and being on the prom com-
mittee. She felt that she was at her best when she was
busy. But if she had homework in more than two
classes in a given class, Natasha felt overwhelmed.

Some people panic in emergency situations. They
get frightened and can't think clearly. They don't
know how to handle the stress of the situation. Others
are calm, seem to know how to help, and are willing
to take charge.

You Can Learn to Manage Stress

How stressful your life is depends on how you *react* to pressure. If you learn to control the way you react, you can learn to manage stress. The stress will work *for* you rather than *against* you. It will help you become a more productive person.

Every day when Ginny came home from school, she would have a snack, listen to music, and watch TV. Just as she was ready to start her homework, her younger brothers would arrive. They were hungry and full of energy. It was Ginny's job to take care of them until their mother got home at 6 o'clock. They wanted her full attention. It was impossible to concentrate on her schoolwork when the noisy boys were around.

Ginny had tough courses. It made her nervous to wait until after dinner to do her homework. Every day was stressful until Ginny learned how to manage the pressure. Instead of relaxing when she got home, she immediately started her homework. By the time her brothers arrived, much of her homework was done. She was ready to deal with them! By changing her schedule slightly, Ginny had learned to manage stress. Starting her homework earlier meant that she had some free time at night, too. Ginny had learned to make stress work for her.

There are many different ways to manage stress. What works for one person may not work for another, but each of us *can* learn to do it.

The Worry Wart

It is not necessarily a bad thing to worry. When we worry, we think ahead to problems that might occur and try to find solutions.

Some people, however, worry about *everything,* even when there's no reason. We call those people "worry warts." The worry warts invite stress. They may create or exaggerate their problems.

"Good" productive worriers look at ways they can change a stressful situation. They take control. They don't sit back and wait for the worst to happen. By taking charge, they are managing stress. They are turning it to their advantage. In the end, their concern helps them instead of becoming a burden.

Myths and Truths about Stress

Myth: The best way to deal with stress is to remove it from your life.

Truth: Stress is a permanent part of life. It will not go away. The best way to deal with it is to learn how to manage it, make it work *for* you, not *against* you.

Myth: Nervous people lead stressful lives.

Truth: Some people are more prone to stress than others. But anyone can learn to manage stress. Just because you are uneasy doesn't mean you will always be stressed out.

Myth: Strong people don't let stress get them down.

Budgeting your time may help to manage your stress.

Truth: Stress is not a sign of weakness. Stress is a part of every person's life. Adults as well as children must learn how to manage stress.

Myth: Once you learn the rules, managing stress will never be a problem.

Truth: Every kind of stress is different. Managing stress at home with your parents is different from dealing with stress at school. What works in one situation may not work in the next. But learning how to manage one type of stress may help you to manage other kinds of stress as well.

High-stress teenagers tend to be loners.

Chapter 2

At Risk for Stress

People are not born with "high-stress" or "low-stress" personalities. But some people are at a higher risk for stress than others. The following questions will help you evaluate whether you are at risk for stress.

- Do you get frustrated easily?
- Do you feel that other people can do things better than you most of the time?
- Does it seem like you're always working but never finishing your work?
- Do you often feel left out or alone?
- Are you depressed?
- Do you worry a lot?
- Have you had any major changes in your life during the past year?

If you answered "yes" to most of these questions, you are at risk for stress. Even if you're at risk for stress, you can learn how to manage it.

Stress and Illness

Doctors believe that there is a link between stress

15

and illness. People who are easily stressed are more likely to get sick than the average person. Headaches, insomnia (having trouble falling or staying asleep), skin rashes, colds, the flu, stomachaches, cold sores, and a loss or increase in appetite are all possible reactions to stress.

A Healthy Diet

Eating a healthy diet is a good way to help manage stress. Some foods increase your chances for feeling stress. Foods that have caffeine or a lot of sugar can cause hyperactivity in some people. Hyperactivity is a state of nervousness that makes it hard for a person to sit still and concentrate. Among the best stress-reducing foods are fresh fruits and vegetables and chicken soup.

Keeping a Regular Schedule

Another way to help manage stress is to keep a regular schedule. Good stress managers set up patterns in their daily lives. They plan their day in advance rather than living from minute to minute. They have a regular schedule for certain activities, including eating and sleeping. Going too long without food and rest can make a person irritable. In this mood, stress is very hard to handle.

Being overtired only makes matters worse. To help reduce stress, it's important to go to bed and get up at about the same time every day.

It's also important to set aside time for relaxing with a quiet activity such as reading or listening to music.

A healthy diet is an important part of feeling good and reducing stress.

Exercise

Exercising is another way to manage stress. It helps to spend 15 to 30 minutes a day doing exercises that require deep breathing, like running or speed walking.

Setting Goals

It is important to be able to set and meet goals. Not being able to make a decision can cause a great deal of stress in a person's life. Indecision can lead to frustration. Nothing can get done or move forward if you don't know what you want to do. If you don't know where you're going, you can't plan how to get there. Gradually, your frustration can lead to depression.

Good stress managers know where they are headed and what they are trying to accomplish. When they meet their goals, they reduce the frustration in their lives and reduce stress.

Talking It Out

High-stress people often choose not to talk about their problems. They may have few close friends or feel as though no one wants to listen. But keeping problems to yourself only makes the problems larger and worse.

Telling someone about what's bothering you can be scary, but it can also help reduce stress. That one good friend may help you find a way to laugh about your troubles. What seems like a disaster at first may not sound nearly as bad when the two of you talk it over.

If you don't feel comfortable talking to a friend about your problems, there are many other people who are available to listen. A family member, favorite teacher, guidance counselor, priest, or rabbi are all good choices. Find someone that you feel comfortable with.

Chapter 3

How to Tell When You're "Stressed-Out"

Does *anxiety* or nervousness over an important exam make you a high-stress person? When you worry the night before a big game, does it mean you're stressed-out? Probably not. You're more likely feeling *tension*. Tension is not the same as stress. Tension is a tightening of the body's muscles. It's what makes the knot in your stomach before opening night of the school play. When your body muscles are tense, it is hard to relax.

Stress is a larger condition. It's a general state of nervousness that can stay with you for long periods of time. Constant tension can lead to stress. People who have trouble relaxing often get stressed-out more easily.

What Are the Warning Signs of Stress?

There are many different ways to spot stress. Not all stress sufferers will have all of these signs, but they will have some of them:

- Headache, chest pain, dizziness, weakness
- Upset stomach, hiccoughs, diarrhea
- Tightness or twitching of muscles
- Grinding of teeth
- Frequent illness or complaints about pain
- Nail biting, hair pulling, or similar behavior
- Changes in sleeping or eating habits
- Constant tiredness or irritability
- Problems concentrating.

Fight or Flight

Thousands of years ago, people lived in caves and hunted with spears. Back then, there were two reactions to stress: fight or flight. If you saw a dangerous animal and you had your spear handy, you could fight. But if it took you by surprise, you might choose flight and take off running.

This *fight-or-flight response* has followed human beings into modern times. Today, when we face stress, our bodies react in much the same way. The brain sounds the alarm when a stressful event happens and says, "You have a problem. What do you want to do, flee or fight back?" The body reacts by producing chemicals that will help it to run or resist. If the stress is not relieved, the body may become *exhausted*.

A nervous habit, like nail biting, may be a sign of stress.

The Fight Reaction

Many times a fight reaction is violent. But violence is not the only way to resist. Lisa's parents had grounded her for coming home late on Friday. Lisa thought she was being treated unfairly. The next morning she came to breakfast in a very bad mood. She would not speak to anyone and refused to do her weekend chores. Every time her mother was near, Lisa would slam doors and swear to herself. Lisa was fighting back in a nonviolent way.

There are many kinds of fight reactions. You may have used some yourself.

- Arguing, rudeness, temper tantrums
- Defying authority—resist or oppose those in charge; see what you can get away with
- Self-destructive behavior—hurting yourself on purpose
- Stealing or cheating.

The Flight Reaction

Some people are born "fighters." Others just want to run away when things get tense.

Alex came from an abusive home, where anger and violence were common. The constant arguing he grew up with caused him to hate fighting. When Alex felt stressed out, he would grab his Walkman and head for the old shed at the end of the block. Sometimes he would stay there all day.

Here are other ways that young people often "take flight":

- Sleep for long periods of time
- Withdraw, becoming quiet
- Work extremely long and hard at a job or project
- Act in negative adult ways (smoking, drinking, using drugs, sexual activity)
- Play with guns, real or imaginary
- Lie, tease, or blame others
- Show a strong interest in the supernatural
- Eat too much or starve oneself.

How Your Body Prepares for Fight or Flight

When Yolanda got off the bus in front of her house, she knew at once that something was wrong. An ambulance was parked outside. The front door was wide open. Immediately Yolanda's heart started beating faster. Her blood pressure increased. She caught her breath, then caught it again. It was hard to breathe normally. The palms of her hands felt cold and sweaty.

Inside Yolanda's body, hormones—chemicals like adrenaline—were being released. The color drained from her face as she walked through the door and saw her father lying on the floor with his eyes closed. Although the room was noisy, Yolanda's hearing became very keen and sharp. "Heart attack," a medic said softly. But the words boomed in Yolanda's ears.

On the bus, Yolanda had been tired and hungry. Now she felt neither. Her stomach tightened up into

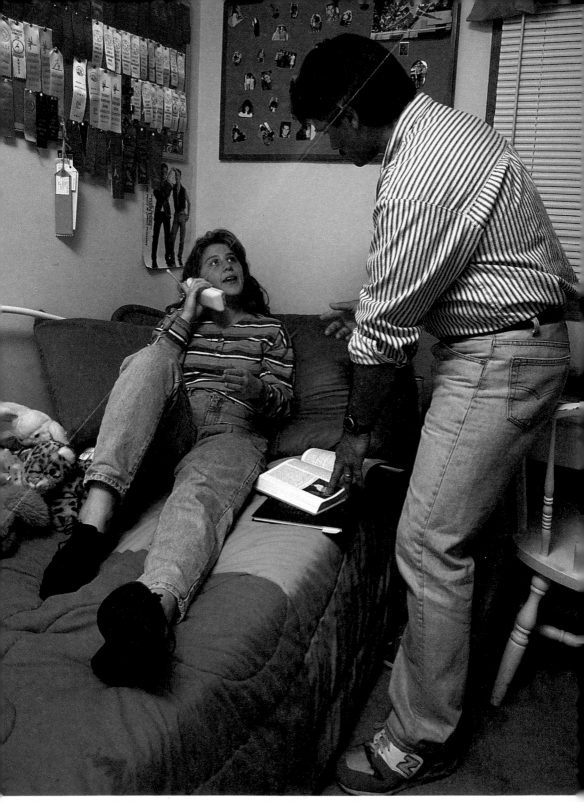

Frequent arguing may be the result of too much stress.

a knot. She felt as if her heart was pounding out of control. She could barely hear her mom telling her to look after her younger sister while she went to the hospital. Only after the ambulance pulled away with her mom and dad did Yolanda notice her headache.

Yolanda's body was reacting to stress. The hormones, or chemicals, that it released were preparing her for fight or flight. All these responses are normal. They happen immediately when a person is in a stressful situation. Once the stressful situation is over, the symptoms go away.

Hurting Your Body

When the human body is under constant stress, it gets weak. It is less able to fight off illness or disease. The longer a person suffers from stress, the greater his or her chances are of becoming ill.

A person who is stressed may feel tired and unable to think clearly. Simple decisions seem overwhelming. Exhaustion makes the person irritable. Many people develop ulcers—sores on the stomach lining. Others develop jaw pains and toothaches from grinding their teeth. Still others may develop nervous twitches, depression, insomnia, high blood pressure, arthritis, cancer, or heart disease. Left untreated, stress can be fatal for some people.

When you constantly misplace your things, you add to your stress.

Chapter 4

Learning About Stressors

A stressor is a cause of stress, something that is threatening to a person. This can be a physical or mental condition, an event, another person, or the person himself. We all have little irritations that bring us distress, such as being in the slowest checkout line in a store. But stressors are the cause of ongoing, long-term stress, the kind that doesn't go away over night.

Stressors Change as We Change

Our stressors change as we get older. Preschool children are often afraid of the dark, which makes bedtime stressful. A first grader may be shy and afraid to leave home. For her or him, going to school is stressful.

27

There are many types of stressors in a teen's life. Some of the more common stressors are:

- *Families:* Arguments with brothers, sisters, parents, stepparents
- *School:* Pressure to get good grades, obeying the rules, respecting authority, avoiding potentially dangerous situations, such as those involving drugs or weapons
- *Peers:* Fitting in, forming close friendships, boyfriend/girlfriend relationships; peer pressure to try drugs or alcohol or engage in sexual activity
- *Changing bodies:* Sexual development, changes in height, weight, body shape, and self-image

Sometimes our stressors are more serious, life-changing events. Studies show that the following can be the most critical stressors in a teenager's life:

- Your parents separate or divorce
- A parent or sibling dies
- You learn that you are pregnant (unmarried girl)
- You learn that you are going to be a father (unmarried boy)
- You are born with or develop a handicap or scar that others can see
- One of your parents goes to jail
- You or a close friend start using drugs or alcohol
- You discover that you are adopted.

If any of these events have happened to you during the past year, you are probably living under great stress.

Unexpected bad news could be the beginning of long-term stress.

You've probably been sick more often than normal. These are major events that make permanent changes in your life.

But it doesn't always take such drastic events to bring on stress. Lesser events can also be the cause of major stress. You are probably living under stress if you have had one or more of these things happen to you recently:

- A change in the way your friends feel about you, either good or bad
- You are suspended from school
- A divorced parent remarries
- You are put in the hospital
- You begin dating, or your friends begin dating and you don't
- A parent goes to the hospital
- You change schools
- A sibling is born or adopted
- A sibling moves out of the house.

Talking things over with a friend may help you relax and feel better.

Fear and Stress

In a speech he gave on the day he became President of the United States, Franklin D. Roosevelt said, "The only thing we have to fear is fear itself." It's true. Often, being afraid of what might happen is much more stressful than what actually does happen.

Many of us worry for days before we go to the dentist. We remember some pain from an earlier time and worry that every visit will hurt. Yet most of the time, there is little or no pain. It is the fear of the pain, not the pain itself, that is the stressor.

Controlling fear can help control stress. But to control fear, we must decide exactly what is causing it and face it head-on. Talk about your fear. Understand it. See how people who once shared your fear have overcome it. Put yourself in situations where you must face your fear and practice how you will handle it.

You May Be Your Worst Stressor

Michael was angry because the director of the school play said he needed to work on his lines. So Michael refused to go to rehearsals for a week. He worried because he knew he was missing valuable practice time, but he didn't want to give the director the satisfaction of being right. On opening night, Michael was so nervous he forgot many of his lines. After the show, he felt even worse because he knew it was his own fault.

Stress is not always someone else's fault. Often, we blame an outside source for our troubles when we are really the cause. Michael's stress was mainly caused by his own stubbornness and unpreparedness. He let the anger he felt toward the director prevent him from doing what he needed to do—practice. Stressors are not always things that happen to us. Many times, stress is caused by how we react to our stressors.

Realistic Ideas

Another source of stress is living with unrealistic ideas about life. Do you have any of these ideas?

I can do anything I set my mind to do. We all have strengths and talents. One person is a great athlete. Another is a math whiz. It's good to set high standards for ourselves and try new things. But it's also wise to remember that none of us are going to be great at everything. Sometimes even a lot of hard work does not guarantee the results we want.

What's the point of trying? I'm only going to fail. Sometimes it seems that no matter what you do, it's never right—you can never please your parents, your teachers, or whoever is important in your life. It's stressful to think of yourself as a failure. So, start talking positively to yourself. Failing at something does not mean that you are a failure. It only means that you're human.

That's not fair! You and a friend were passing notes in class. You got detention, but she didn't. "It's just not fair!" you complain. Maybe not, but many things in life aren't fair. If you realize this, it is easier not to feel like a victim or get stressed out about the situation.

Chapter 5

Dealing with Your Stressor(s)

*W*henever Ken had to speak in front of a group, he got very nervous. His face turned red. His palms got sweaty. His heart started pounding. The group didn't have to be large. Just participating in his counseling group with five other boys was stressful for Ken. It wasn't really speaking that terrified him. It was the thought of speaking.

One day, Ken decided to tackle his stressor. Each boy in the group was asked to name one thing that he disliked about himself. Ken spoke first (something he had never done before). He explained his fear of speaking. To his surprise, two other boys also admitted that they were afraid to speak out in a group. It helped Ken to realize he was not alone.

All the boys agreed that their fear was silly—but real. They made a pact. Every time the group met, one of the three would speak first. All promised to participate at every meeting. When they spoke, they had to tell whether or not their palms were sweaty. They had to admit if their mouths were dry or their hearts were racing. In just a short time, Ken began to feel more confident about public speaking. By tackling his stressor and facing his fear head-on, he was learning to manage stress.

How Do You Want Things to Change?

Knowing the reason for your stress is just the first step. In order to deal with your stressor, you must know what it is you want to change and what you want the *outcome* to be.

Sarah couldn't refuse whenever someone asked her to baby-sit. "Oh, I'll get my schoolwork done," she'd tell herself. But as Sarah's schedule filled up, her grades dropped. She had arguments with her father and disagreements with her teachers. Every day she woke up with a headache or a stomach-ache. Some nights she didn't sleep at all.

Finally, Sarah could live with the stress no longer, so she talked things over with her mother. They decided that Sarah needed to change her schedule to improve her grades. If her grades went up, Sarah's father and teachers would not be so upset. Cutting down on the arguments would help to relieve Sarah's stress.

Overcoming stress means recognizing and dealing with the very things (or persons) that you fear the most.

Making a Step-by-Step Plan

After deciding what she needed to change, Sarah also needed to make a plan. Her plan must cover her entire schedule. First, she made a list of possible solutions, then she looked at the outcome of each idea.

At last, Sarah was ready to make some choices. She found a calendar. Each day for a full week, she wrote down what she planned to do after school. Beside each activity she put the amount of time it would take. When she saw her plan on paper, Sarah realized why she had been so distressed. She only had time for baby-sitting two nights a week— she had been working nearly every night.

Making Your Plan Work

Sarah now practiced her plan. She imagined what she would say when her best customer, Mrs. Grant, asked her to baby-sit.

It was hard at first, saying no. But Sarah knew that to manage the stress in her life, she *must* make her plan work. She must be firm.

With her new schedule, Sarah found she was able to do her homework, get good grades, keep up her other activities, and still do some baby-sitting. Her father was pleased, and the two of them argued less. Managing her time well also made Sarah feel much better about herself. It increased her self-esteem. Her plan had worked to reduce the stress in her life.

Chapter 6

Reducing Stress by Changing Your Behavior

W e live in a time of experts. For every problem, there is a specialist who is knowledgeable and available to help us. But we should not lose faith in ourselves. Just because we're not equipped with special training doesn't mean that we can't solve problems.

In fact, when it comes to managing stress in our lives, *we* are the experts. By changing our behavior, we can reduce stress. It doesn't necessarily take a specialist. It just takes being strict with ourselves. We have to admit that some of the changes may be unpleasant but helpful.

Get Organized

How many times have you needed something in a hurry, like your baseball glove or your left shoe. You *know* it's in your room, but you just can't find it. Five minutes after you leave the house, mom finds it—under the bedspread on your floor. If you had made your bed and picked up your room, you would have found what you needed and saved yourself from another stressful situation.

Here are a few simple tips for reducing minor stress by changing your behavior:

Pick up. Whether it's your desk, your locker, your bedroom, or the garage, keep your things picked up and organized. Put things away after you use them. You'll save time and aggravation the next time you need them.

Make lists. Once a week or once a day, make a list of your activities—homework, entertainment, practice, jobs, etc. When you complete a task, check it off. It's very satisfying to cross finished chores off your list.

Keep a calendar. Hang a calendar in your room. Write on it the times and places for events you have coming up, and phone numbers of persons you need to contact.

Reserve a special place for important items. A desk drawer, a bulletin board, or even an old shoe box will do. Here you can keep notices, schedules, and information that you may need to refer to at a later time.

Taking a little time to keep yourself organized can reduce minor stress.

Throw things away. Wage war on clutter! Don't "clean" your room by scooping up the clutter and stuffing it in a corner. Sort through it. Keep what you need and throw the rest away.

Be a Good Time Manager

Many adults have never learned to manage their time properly. They rush from one activity to the next. They're tense, nervous, on edge, and always complaining about how much they have to do.

Manage your time well so you won't lead a stressed-out life. Take a few minutes to list your daily activities. Beside each activity, write the amount of time you expect it to take.

Try to make your schedule realistic. Be sure you leave time each day for being with friends, relaxing, and doing things you enjoy. Allowing for free time is a very important part of managing stress.

Some Dos and Don'ts

Don't try to be all things to all people. You can't be a star athlete, get straight A's, hold down a job after school, volunteer at church, and be a friend to everyone in town. You're only one person. Others may admire you for trying to be superteen, but they don't have to live with your stress. Be honest. Know when to say, "I have to slow down."

Be able to judge your risks. If we don't take risks, we'd never make progress. But ask yourself how important the activity really is. Maybe it's worth the risk, the tension, the stress. Maybe it isn't. There's a difference between taking *calculated risks* (those you have decided are worth a chance) and being foolish.

Think positively. People who see the dark side of everything are usually stress-prone. When an idea is suggested, they immediately think of reasons why it won't work. Negative thinkers tend to be depressed. They take the joy out of life. They are afraid to take risks that will improve their lives, because they feel that their lives are out of their control.

On the other hand, think about the people you know who are always "up" and live each day to the fullest. They have more friends than the negative thinkers, because people enjoy being around them. They have confidence in themselves and in their ability to control their lives. If they should fail at something, their world does not come to an end. They accept their mistakes and try to learn from them. Generally, a positive person has a good sense of humor—a great way to relieve the tension that can lead to stress.

Don't waste time worrying about things you can't change. Positive people are rarely overcome with worry. If there's nothing they can do to change or improve a situation, they accept it and move on. They focus instead on those things over which they have some control.

Don't turn to drugs or alcohol to help you deal with stress. When a person is having a particularly bad or stressful time, they are more susceptible to offers of drugs or alcohol. You may hear that smoking marijuana or drinking a few beers will help you forget about your problems and your stress. That may be true temporarily, but when you come down off the high or sober up, the problems, and the stress, will still be there. And now they'll be even worse because you have to worry about being caught drinking or doing drugs. Using drugs or alcohol is never a solution. It only increases the number of problems.

Change your diet. Certain foods or drinks can greatly increase a person's level of stress. Some also promote poor health, both physical and mental. Cutting down on these items, or removing them completely from your diet, can help reduce stress.

- *Sugar*—sweet desserts, gum, ice cream, candy, sweet cereal, cookies
- *Salt*—fast food, packaged food, lunch meat, canned soup
- *Caffeine*—tea, coffee, colas, chocolate
- *Additives*—MSG, BVO, sugar substitutes, artificial coloring, etc. Look for these and other additives on the labels of foods like white bread, processed cheese spread, prepackaged foods, and fast food.

Chapter 7

Mind Over Matter

Art Kiev is a *therapist* who works with teenagers suffering from stress and depression. In his book *Riding Through the Downers, Hassles, Snags & Funks*, he says that reducing stress depends on how *you* handle a situation. "It may be unpleasant for you to hear that the problem is in your hands," he warns. "But if you learn to control your reactions, situations that once seemed impossible will begin to look like challenges, not obstacles."

Sure, you say, that may be true. But how do I learn to control my reactions? How do I turn an obstacle into a challenge?

You're in Charge

Start by telling yourself, "It's up to me. I'm in charge here." Don't look for someone to blame for your stress. Don't look for someone to help you out of it. Rely on yourself.

"Other people and events and things do not stress you," says Dr. M.W. Buckalew, who teaches classes on stress management. *"YOU* stress you." In his book *Learning to Control Stress*, Dr. Buckalew says that if you talk properly to yourself, you will not get angry as often. You will start to see things in a different way. He suggests five ways of talking properly to yourself:

Take responsibility for what has happened. Say, "I made myself so mad," not, "He made me so mad."

Don't label yourself. Stop calling yourself shy, clumsy, stupid, etc. Instead, talk about your behavior. "That decision I made was really dumb," not, *"I'm* so dumb." Or, "During the game my running was clumsy," instead of, *"I'm* so clumsy."

Stop generalizing. Avoid talking about "them" or "they" when you really mean one particular person. You may not get along well with your English teacher. But that doesn't mean that *all* teachers are difficult. Don't let one bad experience ruin an activity forever. Instead of saying, "I'm just no good at music," say, "This piece is really tough, but I know I can learn it if I keep practicing."

Don't set yourself up for failure. It's good to have high ideals. But don't set goals that are impossible to meet. You'll quickly become frustrated. The frustration will lead to a lack of *self-confidence.*

Give yourself constructive criticism. Instead of grumbling that you're a failure, look closely at what you've done wrong and see how you can improve.

Create a positive, successful picture of yourself before you enter a stressful situation.

Things You Can Do to Break the Tension

Psych up. Get excited about an event that you expect to be stressful. Instead of worrying about it, look forward to it. Think of how it will be interesting, fun, or different. Talk to yourself in a positive way about this new experience.

Psych down. Relax. Don't run on nervous energy. Force yourself to stop and look at the situation with a clear head. Spend some quiet time talking to yourself about how you will handle this stressor.

Stay calm. At first, this may seem unnatural, like you're putting on an act. But the longer you put on that act, the more natural it becomes. Soon you *will* be calm.

Take a break. Sometimes the best way to relieve stress is to walk away for a little while. Change the scene. In a different place, your stressor may suddenly seem much less important.

Finish tasks. Often we invite stress by never finishing what we start. We think of ourselves as failures because we don't accomplish our goals, even the simple ones. Break the stress by getting out your chore chart and doing at least two of those jobs—right now!

Write it down! Writing is a great form of stress relief. Keep a journal or write a letter to yourself when you get frustrated or upset.

Be kind. Say or do something nice for someone else today. It will make you feel good about yourself. Your positive self-image will help reduce stress in your own life.

Building a Positive Self-Image

How do you prepare to handle a stressful situation? Try painting a positive mental picture. Think about an event you have coming up that you expect to be stressful. Picture the place where that event will happen. Fill your picture with all the people you expect to be there, including yourself. See yourself moving and speaking confidently as if you are playing a part in a play. The clearer and more detailed your picture, the more it will help you.

Olivia admired Regina. Regina always knew what to say around people. She seemed sure of herself without being "stuck up." Olivia was tired of being called "the shy, quiet type." She made up her mind to try to be more like Regina. She was determined to become more outgoing.

Olivia was worried about the junior prom, two weeks away. She was pleased that Eddie had asked her, but frightened and stressed by the thought of going. What would they talk about? How would she look in her new dress? What would she say to Eddie's friends? Would they like her?

Then Olivia remembered her plan. To help relieve her stress, she went to the gym where the dance would be held. She stood in the empty room, picturing the decorations, the music, herself and Eddie, their friends, even Regina and her date.

For the next two weeks, she "rehearsed" the prom in her mind. The first time she rehearsed, she was a shy, tongue-tied, self-conscious teen. But each day her mental picture became more positive. By the time prom night came, Olivia was ready. She felt little stress because she had practiced this night so many times in her mind. The practice had helped her build a positive self-image—Olivia had a great time at the dance.

Crying is nature's way to reduce stress.

Chapter 8

Relieving Stress Through Your Body

*M*ike sat on the couch, watching his two-year-old sister kick, scream, throw her arms around, and turn bright red. The little girl was having a temper tantrum. Their brother had just grabbed her stuffed bear and run out of the room. Mike knew how she felt. Just this morning, the same brother had spilled a whole pitcher of lemonade on Mike's collection of baseball cards. He had felt like crying and screaming, too.

But Mike was the oldest child, 11 next month. Big boys don't cry—at least that's what he learned somewhere. No one expected him to cry. Crying was for sissies. Right?

Wrong. Crying is one of the best ways to relieve stress at any age. Crying forces us to breathe deeply. When we breathe deeply, our bodies begin to relax and the stress is relieved.

The Importance of Deep Breathing

During deep breathing, the heart rate slows down. The flight-or-fight response is turned off. Relaxation begins. How can you learn to control your breathing when you're under stress?

Count to ten. Don't follow that urge to punch someone or scream in his or her face. Instead, block everything from your mind. Tell yourself, "I'm not going to argue. I'm going to count very slowly to ten. When I'm through, I'll be in control of myself. Here I go." Then begin counting slowly—one... two... three... By the time you reach ten, you'll be calm enough to take the next step.

Slow your breathing. A person under stress takes fast, short, shallow breaths, almost like gasps. Force yourself instead to take long, deep breaths. Count slowly as you breathe in: "One-thousand-one, one-thousand-two, one-thousand-three." Count the same way when you breathe out.

Wait a second. Pause after you breathe out. Don't actually hold your breath. Just stop before your next breath. When you do inhale, make it a normal breath, not a gasp. Continue breathing this way for several minutes, pausing before drawing each new breath.

Stop tightening your muscles. Don't grind your jaws together. Don't even let your top teeth touch the bottom. Shake your arms loosely from the shoulders. Shake your hands gently from the wrists.

Training Your Body to Relax

The religious masters of India have taught the rest of the world two very good ways to overcome stress. One is *yoga.* Yoga is a mystic Hindu discipline. There are many yoga exercises, all designed to relax the body. There are many books that can show you different yoga positions. The most common one is sitting on the floor, back straight, legs crossed with feet on thighs. Arms are held out in front of the body. In this position, begin deep breathing. Concentrate only on being quiet and relaxed. Stay in this position for several minutes, thinking about your breathing.

Meditation is the other excellent way to relieve stress. But to do it you must sit still and concentrate very hard. Find a comfortable position in a quiet room. Lying on the floor on your back is good. Focus on something simple, like the rhythm of your own heartbeat. Or slowly repeat a quiet, easy sound like *awww-uhm.* Block out all other sights and sounds. Concentrate on your object. Soon your body will begin to relax. A soothing feeling will wash over you.

In recent years, relaxation tapes have become a popular way to relieve stress. Some doctors and dentists even use them when they are working on patients. You can buy these tapes in a music store or borrow them from the library. They play sounds from nature, like waterfalls, wind blowing, and birds chirping. Soft, soothing music runs behind the sounds. Find a quiet, comfortable place to listen to your tape. You'll be amazed at how quickly you begin to relax.

Working Off Stress Through Exercise

Shawn has a punching bag hanging in his base-ment. When he is under stress, he heads for it. "I love the relief I get from hitting that bag. I work up a sweat and breathe hard. Sometimes I talk to myself. When I'm done, I just collapse on a mat I keep beside my bag. Sometimes I'm so relaxed, I even fall asleep."

There are many ways to relieve stress through exercise. You can run, swim, jump rope, play ten-nis, or just walk. Exercise helps loosen up your muscles. When your muscles are relaxed, stress is relieved. Exercise also helps focus your attention on something other than your stressor. When you're concentrating on a tennis ball, for example, you forget how upset you are with your girlfriend. When you're jogging or walking, the new scenery helps you forget your problems at home.

Setting a regular exercise time each day helps to reduce stress. It also gets the body in shape for handling long-term stress, the kind that doesn't go

A regular exercise program is a healthy way to relieve stress.

A good listener can be a valuable friend.

away when your temper cools down. Be sure to choose exercises that you like. Otherwise, the exercise time will only add more stress to your life. Remember, this doesn't have to be a bodybuilding program. It is a program to reduce stress.

Helping Other People Overcome Stress

It may not be you who's tied up in knots and all stressed out. Maybe it's your friend, your sister or brother, your mother or father. You can help that person relieve stress with a few simple actions.

Touching. Don't be afraid to give someone a squeeze, a hug, a kiss, a pat on the back. Touching does three important things. It helps the other person relax. It shows them you care. It makes them feel good to know that someone else understands what they are going through.

Laughing. Smiles are catching! You can help relieve a friend's stress by putting on a happy face yourself. Sometimes you don't have to say a word. Laughter is a great stress breaker. It relieves the tension in a person's body and starts the process of relaxation.

Listening. Being quiet is the first step toward relaxing. You can help a friend overcome stress by being quiet yourself. Let him or her do the talking. When you do respond, be brief and calm. Sit together quietly and listen to soft music. Or just sit in silence. A *really* good friend is one you can be with for a long time without needing to talk.

Chapter 9

You're in Control

When you feel as though your life is crazy and you're completely stressed-out, take a deep breath and say to yourself, "I'm in control."

You have the skills you need to manage the stress in your life. You just need to use them. Knowing your strengths and weaknesses, setting realistic goals, and establishing an outlet for your stress are all good ways to cope with stress.

Don't fall into the trap of "the easy out." These outs can include using drugs or alcohol, ignoring your responsibilities, avoiding the people who cause you stress, or not dealing with the stress. These things will only make your stress, and your life, worse. You need to deal with your stressors head-on. You can't do this if you're drunk, high, or avoiding life.

Learning to relax can keep you in control of your body and your mind.

Four things can help you take control of your life. *There is good in every situation.* Look for that good point when things seem to be going bad. For example, maybe your mom and dad are fighting again, but you're going to spend the night at a friend's house. Finding the good will help you think positively, which will put you in a better frame of mind to manage your stress.

Things could be worse. Sometimes it helps to figure out just how they might be worse. Suzanne's parents were divorced. Suzanne was disappointed that she had to visit her dad this weekend rather than going out with her friends. Then she thought about her friend, Rosie. Rosie's dad left when Rosie was just a baby. She never got to see her dad. Suzanne realized that she was lucky to be able to see her dad regularly. She pulled out her weekend bag and started packing.

Most problems have solutions. Stress sometimes builds because you can't see the answers to your problems. Things seem hopeless. But by having confidence in yourself and believing in yourself, you have the tools you need to take control and find a solution.

Time heals all wounds. No matter how bad things may be, no matter how great the stress, things will seem better after some time has passed. The stress you feel because of the death of a relative or a close friend may last for months. But once you have learned to manage the stress, you'll be able to focus on the positive things in your life once again.

Once you accept that stress will always be a part of your life, you can concentrate on your reactions to stress and stressors. Stress will take a backseat, and you will be ready to face life and all its challenges.

Glossary

additive A material, often a chemical, added to a product to improve or change it.

adrenaline Hormone that stimulates the heart and speeds up the body's activity.

alcohol A substanace, usually found in liquor, that changes the way a person thinks and acts.

anxiety Feeling of worry or nervousness.

caffeine Stimulant found in coffee, chocolate, and other food items that excites the brain and nervous system.

calculated risk Hazard or risk whose chance of failure or success has been judged before taking any action.

confident Sure, certain, full of faith.

control To take responsibility for your actions.

depressed Overcome by a feeling of gloom or deep sadness.

destiny A person's future; what happens to him or her over time.

distress State of pain, suffering, danger, or trouble.

exhaustion State of being extremely weak or tired.

fight-or-flight response The way the body reacts
    to stress by producing chemicals and sending mes-
    sages to the brain that prepare a person to fight or
    run from the stressor.

hormones Chemicals in the glands that help the
    body grow, stay in balance, and react to outside
    stimulants.

hyperactivity More activity or movement than
    average.

irritable Impatient, angry; in a bad mood that
    makes one very sensitive.

marijuana A drug that slows down a person's body
    and makes him or her see things that aren't there.

meditation Mental exercise that focuses deeply on a
    single idea, thought, or object.

outcome The result of taking action.

self-confidence Trust or faith in oneself.

self-destructive To be harmful to oneself.

self-esteem How a person feels about himself or
    herself.

stressed out Overcome by stress.

stressor A cause of stress.

tension Mental strain, worry; a feeling of being
    pulled from different directions.

therapist Person specially trained to treat a disease
    or mental condition.

Where to Go for Help

The first step in managing your stress is to let an adult know that you are having trouble. If your own parent cannot help, talk to a school counselor, social worker, religious leader, or a friend's parent.

If you think you may need more help, there are other places to look. Most communities have mental health centers, clinics, or hospitals that deal with stress-related problems. To find a clinic in your town or city, look in the Yellow Pages under "Stress Management" or "Mental Health Services." Asking for help in managing your stress is not a sign of weakness. It is a sign of strength and courage. It means that you care enough to help yourself. Below are some national organizations that deal with stress management:

American Institute of Stress
124 Park Avenue
Yonkers, NY 10703
(914) 963-1200

Capable Kids and Families
  Counseling Centers
1615 Orrington Avenue
Evanston, IL 60201
(847) 866-7335

The Hardiness Institute
19742 MacArthur
  Boulevard
Irvine, CA 92715-2408
(714) 252-0580

In Canada
Canadian Mental Health
  Association
2160 Yonge Street
Toronto, Ontario M4S 2Z3
(416) 484-7750

For Further Reading

Atkins, Andrea. "School Stress." *Better Homes and Gardens,* November 1991, pages 37–38.

Gallo, Nick. "Calming Jangled Nerves." *Better Homes and Gardens,* August 1991, pages 163–164.

Kiev, Ati. *Riding Through the Downers, Hassles, Snags & Funks.* New York: Elsevier-Dutton, 1980.

Kuczen, Barbara. *Childhood Stress.* New York: Dell Publishing, 1982.

Sapolsky, Robert. "Growing Up in a Hurry." *Discover,* June 1992, pages 40–50.

Saunders, Antoinette, and Remsberg, Bonnie. *The Stress-Proof Child.* New York: Holt, Rinehart and Winston, 1985.

Stark, Elizabeth. "Stress: It's All Relative and Easy to Manage." *American Health,* December 1992, pages 41–47.

Sylvester, Sandra M. *Living with Stress.* Carthage, IL: Good Apple, 1991.

Index

A
additives, 42

B
body (and stress), 51–52
Buckalew, Dr. M.W., 44

C
caffeine, 16, 42
changing behavior, 34, 36–42

D
deep breathing (and stress), 50
depression, 18
diet, stress-reducing, 16, 42

E
exercise (and stress), 52, 55

F
fear, 31
fight-or-flight response, 20, 50
fight reactions, 20, 22, 25
flight reactions, 20, 22–23, 25

H
health problems (stress-
related), 16, 20, 25
helping others (with stress), 55
high-stress people, 15, 18, 19

K
Kieve, Art, 43

L
Learning to Control Stress, 44
low-stress people, 15, 16

M
meditation, 51
myths (about stress), 12–13

P
pressure (reaction to), 10, 11,
32

R
*Riding Through the Downers,
Hassles, Snags &
Funks*, 43
Roosevelt, Franklin D., 31

S
salt, 42
self-esteem (and stress), 10, 36,

56
stress
  defenses against, 10
  definition of, 6
  long-term effects of, 25
  managing, 11–13, 16, 18, 31,
      37
  reducing, 36, 37–38, 40–47,
      50–53, 56–58
  sources of, 32
  statistics on, 7
  tension and, 19, 46
  test, 15
  warning signs of, 20
stress managers, 16–18, 57–58
"stressed -out," 7, 12, 19, 40
stressor(s), 31, 32

dealing with, 34–36
definition of, 28
how to spot a, 28, 29, 30
sugar, 16, 42

T
talking positively (to yourself),
      44
teenagers, causes of stress for,
      27–30
tension breakers, 46

W
"worry-warts," 12

Y
yoga, 51

About the Author

Eleanor H. Ayer is the author of several books for children and young adults. She has written about people of the American West, World War II and modern Europe, and current social issues of interest to teenagers. Her recent topics include depression, teen fatherhood, teen marriage, and teen suicide. Ms. Ayer holds a master's degree from Syracuse University with a specialty in literacy journalism. She lives with her husband and two sons in Colorado.

Photo Credits

Cover photo by Stuart Rabinowitz; all other photographs by Norma Mondazzi.